This book belongs to

_____

Walt Disney®

VOLUME 3

PINOCCHIO'S PROMISE

WALT DISNEY FUN-TO-READ LIBRARY

A BANTAM BOOK

TORONTO • NEW YORK • LONDON • SYDNEY • AUCKLAND

Pinocchio's Promise   A Bantam Book/January 1986   All rights reserved.   Copyright © 1986 Walt Disney Productions.   This book may not be reproduced, in whole or in part, by mimeograph or any other means.

ISBN 0-553-05576-3

Published simultaneously in the United States and Canada.   Bantam Books are published by Bantam Books, Inc.   Its trademark, consisting of the words "Bantam Books" and the portrayal of a rooster, is Registered in U.S. Patent and Trademark Office and in other countries.   Marca Registrada.   Bantam Books, Inc., 666 Fifth Avenue, New York, New York 10103.   Printed in the United States of America   0 9 8 7 6 5 4 3 2 1

One day Geppetto, the woodcarver, finished making a cuckoo clock. He held it up proudly.

"Pinocchio! Jiminy! Come see this beautiful clock! I made it for Mrs. Romano."

"It looks okay," said Pinocchio.

"My poor boy, you are so bored while I work," said Geppetto. "But now I have some work for you."

"Take this clock to Mrs. Romano. Then come home as fast as you can. Promise?"
"I promise!" said Pinocchio.

He took the clock and skipped away.
Pinocchio did not see Gideon and
Foulfellow. But they saw him—and the clock.

"That is one beautiful clock," said Gideon.
"It must be worth a lot of money," said
Foulfellow. "How can we get our hands on it?"

Pinocchio stopped to read a circus poster. "I wish I could see the circus," he said aloud.

"My, my," said Foulfellow softly. "Look what we have here." He picked up two old circus tickets from the street. "Let's see if Pinocchio will fall for a little trick!"

"Pinocchio, dear boy!" said Foulfellow. "I have two tickets for the circus. But I cannot go. Would you like to go instead?"

"Oh yes, thank you!" said Pinocchio.

"Pinocchio!" called Jiminy. "What about your promise to Geppetto?"

Pinocchio sighed. "Sorry, I cannot go," he said. "I have to take this clock to Mrs. Romano."

"I will do that," said Foulfellow grandly. "Here are the tickets. Enjoy the circus!"

With that, Foulfellow grabbed the clock. And Gideon pulled Pinocchio off to the circus.

When Pinocchio got to the circus, he did not see Gideon leave him and hide. Pinocchio handed his ticket to the ticket man.

"Why, this is an old ticket! You think you can fool me?" asked the angry ticket man.

In shame, Pinocchio ran through the circus. He just wanted to get away from the ticket man.

Pinocchio ran and ran. Very soon he was lost. And now Jiminy Cricket was nowhere to be found.

Pinocchio stopped to catch his breath.
Whoosh! Suddenly he was covered
with water!
Two huge elephants wanted to play.
Pinocchio ran away, dripping wet.

Next he ran into three happy clowns.
"Let's have some fun!" shouted the
clowns. They picked up Pinocchio. They threw
him up high.

"Help!" shouted Pinocchio.
Just then, a clown threw him <u>way</u> up.
Pinocchio flew through the air.

"Ooof," said Pinocchio. He had landed on the back of a beautiful white horse.

"Stay and ride with me," said the girl on the horse's back.

"No, thank you," said Pinocchio. "I must find Jiminy Cricket."

He jumped off the horse and landed with a thump on the ground.

Then along came the circus strong man.
"What have we got here?" he laughed.

"Please put me down!" cried Pinocchio.
"Okay," said the strong man with a
hearty laugh. Then he dropped Pinocchio
into a pile of hay.

Pinocchio wondered where to go now. He just <u>had</u> to find Jiminy. Suddenly a lion tamer came running out of a nearby tent. Pinocchio heard screams coming from inside.

Pinocchio crept up to the tent. "What is going on in here?" he wondered. Pinocchio crawled all the way into the tent.

Suddenly he heard the roar of a crowd
around him. He was in the middle of a circus
ring. The bright lights made Pinocchio blink.
He did not see the lion, ready to spring.

The lion jumped. He caught Pinocchio in his huge paw. He opened his mouth.
Pinocchio saw the lion's big white teeth.

The lion sniffed at Pinocchio. "Hmm," he thought. "It looks like a little boy. But it smells like wood. Why, it smells just like the old wooden ball I used to play with."

The lion began to purr. He rolled over on
his back. He held Pinocchio in the air. Then
he turned over on his stomach and fell asleep.
The people could not believe their eyes.

Very, very carefully, the ringmaster crept up to the lion. Very, very carefully, he put a collar around the lion's neck.

Then he pulled gently on the collar. The
lion got up. He followed the ringmaster like a
big kitten.

Pinocchio stood up and brushed himself
off. The crowd cheered. Pinocchio did not
know what to do next. He jumped out of the
ring and ran away.

Jiminy Cricket ran after him. "Pinocchio, where have you been? I have been looking for you everywhere."

Just then Pinocchio ran right into the
ringmaster.
"How did you get in that tent?" the
ringmaster asked. "You could have been hurt.
What if the lion had bitten you?"

Pinocchio felt ashamed. He knew that he was just a bad boy. He had gotten into the circus without a ticket. And he was not even supposed to be at the circus!

Pinocchio turned and ran far away. Jiminy
Cricket ran after him.
"Pinocchio!" he called. "Wait for me!
Don't keep running away. Remember your
promise to Geppetto."

"Oh, the clock!" gasped Pinocchio.

"Yes, we must get the clock back from Foulfellow before something terrible happens to it," cried Jiminy.

Pinocchio and Jiminy hurried back to town.

Smack! Pinocchio ran right into a policeman.

"What is your hurry, young man?" asked the policeman.

Pinocchio told the policeman about Foulfellow and the clock.

"I'll bet that rascal Foulfellow is trying to sell it," said the policeman. "Let's get him!"

The policeman blew his whistle. He waved his stick. Pinocchio and Jiminy Cricket followed close behind him.

"There he is!" shouted the policeman. Foulfellow was just about to sell the clock. Then he saw the policeman and Pinocchio running toward him. He threw the clock up in the air and ran.

The policeman chased him. He was still shouting and waving his stick.

Pinocchio jumped and reached for the clock. He caught it just in time.

"Phew, that was close," he sighed. "Let's take the clock to Mrs. Romano right now!"

Mrs. Romano was very happy to see
Pinocchio and her new clock. And Pinocchio
was very happy to give it to her, at last.

When Pinocchio got back, he found
Geppetto waiting in their little house.
"Pinocchio! Where have you been? I was
going to take you and Jiminy to the circus
today. Now it is too late," said Geppetto.

"We stopped to learn a lesson along the way," said Jiminy Cricket. "Next time, we will stick to our promises, won't we, Pinocchio?"

Pinocchio nodded his head. "Next time,
I'll keep my promise—I promise!"